5-23-93

To My Friends at the Fauquier Library,
    Thank you for inviting me! Keep
reading, writing, & drawing!
            Your friend,
            Bonnie-Alise Leggat

PUNT, PASS & POINT!

written & illustrated by
BONNIE-ALISE LEGGAT

LANDMARK EDITIONS, INC.
P.O. Box 4469 • 1402 Kansas Avenue • Kansas City, Missouri 64127
(816) 241-4919

Dedicated to:
Mrs. Aldene Helwick
for being the best
third-grade teacher
a kid could have;
and to my brother Ian
for showing me I could draw.

P.S. Thanks, Mom. I love you!

COPYRIGHT © 1992 BY BONNIE-ALISE LEGGAT

International Standard Book Number: 0-933849-39-7 (LIB.BDG.)

Library of Congress Cataloging-in-Publication Data
Leggat, Bonnie-Alise, 1982-
    Punt, pass & point! / written and illustrated by Bonnie-Alise Leggat.
    p.   cm.
    Summary: When Amy, the only girl and star player on her school's football team, breaks her arm, her parents insist that she give up football and take up ballet instead.
    ISBN 0-933849-39-7 (lib.bdg. : acid free)
    1. Children's writings.   2. Children's art.
    [1. Football—Fiction.   2. Ballet dancing—Fiction.
    3. Self-esteem—Fiction.   4. Sex role—Fiction.
    5. Children's writings.   6. Children's art.]
    I. Title.
    PZ7.L52125Pu   1992
    [E]—dc20

                                    92-17598
                                    CIP
                                    AC

Editorial Coordinator: Nancy R. Thatch
Creative Coordinator: David Melton

Printed in the United States of America

Landmark Editions, Inc.
P.O. Box 4469
1402 Kansas Avenue
Kansas City, Missouri 64127
(816) 241-4919

PUNT, PASS & POINT!

One of the pleasures of publishing books written and illustrated by students is having the opportunity to work with extraordinarily gifted and talented kids.

Bonnie-Alise Leggat is a marvelous author and illustrator! She is a quick thinker, an exceptional writer, and a clever cartoonist.

From the minute Bonnie-Alise entered our offices, she was eager to do whatever was needed to improve her book. Manuscript sessions were lively and rewarding. It was fun to observe her as she utilized her great ideas and wonderful sense of humor to mold and expand her delightful story.

Bonnie-Alise was just as determined to put her best efforts into redoing and refining her art work. As she worked to complete her final illustrations, her drawing skills improved, and she began to add more detail and characters to the scenes she created. As her drawing skills improved, her self-confidence grew stronger. As her self-confidence grew stronger, her illustrations became even more elaborate and humorous.

The result of Bonnie-Alise's best work is PUNT, PASS & POINT!, a hilarious book that will have readers chuckling on one fun-filled page after another.

Now, just turn the page and get ready to start laughing.

— David Melton
Creative Coordinator
Landmark Editions, Inc.

Hi. i am amy.

You probably noticed — i don't capitalize the letter "a" in my name. This is not a mistake. i do it on purpose. i don't capitalize the letter "a" or the letter "i" when i write about myself because i am not an important person — not anymore.

I used to be important. Last year I was the only girl on our school's football team. I was smaller than most of the boys. But I could run faster, jump higher, and catch the ball better than any of them. And I made more touchdowns than all the guys put together.

When I was the star player, I always capitalized my "A" and my "I." But all of that changed after the big game.

Our team is called the Bay City Hotshots. Last year we won every game and made it to the state play-offs. If we could win the final game, we would become the state champions.

Winning that game would not be easy for us because the other team was the Tidewater Tigers. Everyone knew the Tigers were the roughest, toughest team in the junior league. Those guys were so big, they should have been called the "Gorillas."

During the first quarter of the game, the Tigers made two touchdowns. When they got the ball again, their quarterback threw a long forward pass. But before a Tiger could catch the ball, I jumped up and caught it in mid-air.

Our hometown crowd cheered!

I turned and ran toward the goal line as fast as I could — ten yards, twenty yards, thirty yards.

"Run, Amy! Run!" the crowd yelled wildly.

Then it happened — four of the biggest Tigers caught up with me. They dived forward and grabbed my legs. Splat! Then down I went! Crunch!

When the Tigers finally let go of me, I staggered to my feet.

"Are you all right, Amy?" the coach wanted to know.

"I'm fine," I replied.

But I wasn't fine. When I tried to pick up the ball, my right arm wouldn't move. It just hung from my shoulder like a limp rag.

Lights flashed and sirens squealed as I was rushed to the hospital in an ambulance. In the emergency room, a doctor set my broken arm and put a cast on it.

While I rode home in the car with Mom and Dad, I heard the bad news on the radio. The sportscaster's voice blurted out, "The Tidewater Tigers Win 48 to Nothing! The Tigers Are the New State Champions!"

"That's awful!" I groaned. "But, next year our team will beat the stripes off those Tigers."

"There will be no more football for you, young lady," Mom said.

"That's right," Dad agreed. "It's too dangerous."

I argued, begged, and pleaded, but my parents would not change their minds. When I was a home, I stayed in my room most of the time. If Mom or Dad came near, I would heave the saddest sighs possible and make sure I had a gloomy look on my face. I hoped if they saw how unhappy I was, they might drop to their knees and say, "Oh, Amy, please forgive us. We can't stand to see you be so sad. Of course you can play football next year." But that never happened.

Finally, I had to face the facts. Like it or not, I was retired from football. So I hung up my cleats, took down my posters, and packed my uniform, number 13, in mothballs. Then I placed my football on the highest shelf in my closet where I wouldn't have to see it every day.

I felt like a complete failure. I had failed the team, and I had failed myself. At that moment, my capital "I" and my capital "A" were cut down in size.

i began to lose all interest in school. My grades dropped lower and lower, and i stopped talking to my classmates. When i saw any of the guys from the football team in the hallway, i would turn and walk in the other direction.

i wasn't even interested in celebrating on my birthday. i watched glumly as Mom placed my presents in the living room. And then, one big box tied with a blue ribbon caught my attention. It was just the right size to hold a brand new football uniform with shoulder pads and helmet.

"All right!" i told myself. "Mom and Dad have changed

their minds after all." i couldn't wait to open that box and call the coach to tell him, "AMY J. KENDRICK is back on the team!"

After dinner i blew out the candles on my cake and ran to the big package. i pulled off the ribbon, ripped open the paper, and removed the lid. Then i eagerly reached inside, ready to pull out my new uniform.

"WHAT'S THIS!" i exclaimed as i pulled out a blue thing that looked like a tiny pair of panty hose with teeny weeny sleeves.

"It's your leotard, dear," Mom replied.

"*My* leotard? This little thing isn't big enough for a munchkin!"

"It will stretch to fit any size," Mom told me.

"Well, whoop-dee-doo!" i said in disgust as i threw it aside.

Then i took out a pink thing that had ruffles all over it.

"And what's this?" i asked.

"It's a tutu," Mom said.

"A what-what?"

"A tutu," she replied. "It's a little skirt for you to wear over your leotard. Isn't it sweet!"

"Just precious!" i said, clenching my teeth. "It looks like one of Aunt Matilda's old floppy hats."

Then i pulled out a pair of pink slippers and held them up.

"Aren't they cute!" Mom cooed.

"Too cute for words!" i snapped back. "i simply can't wait to wear them when i wade through the mud!"

"I'm glad you like them," Mom said, trying to ignore my snippy remarks. Then she handed an envelope to me.

i hoped i would find money inside. With enough money i could leave home and find parents who really cared about my feelings. i ripped open the envelope and pulled out...a gift certificate. It read:

ONE COMPLETE YEAR
OF DANCE LESSONS
AT
MADAME LEZLIE CAMILLE'S SCHOOL OF BALLET

Believe it or not, i was speechless.

"Amy, ballet lessons will be good for you," Mom explained. "You must learn to walk gracefully and stop charging into a room like a wild buffalo."

"Ballet is for sissies," i replied, "and i'm no sissy. i will NEVER take ballet lessons!"

Famous last words!

On Saturday morning Mom parked the car near Madame Camille's studio. She had to pull me out of the front seat. Then, with my heels scraping along the sidewalk, Mom dragged me toward the building.

"You'll like ballet," Mom told me as she pulled me up, up, up a long flight of stairs. When we finally reached the second floor, she opened the door and pushed me into the studio.

"Behave yourself," Mom instructed. Then she turned her back on me and hurried down the stairs.

There i stood in a huge room, feeling out of place and miserable. At the other end of the room were five students — four girls and one boy. i recognized the girls immediately. All of them attended my school, but they were definitely not my friends.

Elizabeth Ann Witherspoon was one of them. Elizabeth Ann was talking, of course. She talked, talked, talked all the time. She was the school gossip and told everything she heard.

Laura Kluttz was the tallest of the girls. She had long skinny legs, and her knees knocked together when she walked. Maybe that was what made her so clumsy. She was always bumping into things and tripping over her own feet.

It was easy to see Bertha Mae Beeman. Bertha had a bit of a weight problem because she ate too many sweets. i could tell that her leotard was already stretched to the limit. i was certain if she ate one more cupcake that leotard would explode.

Standing in front of the mirror, admiring her own long blonde curls, was Priscilla Snootman. i've always called her "Priscilla Priss" because she thinks she's perfect in every way. What a stuck-up snob!

When the girls saw me, Priscilla stuck her nose even higher in the air. Elizabeth Ann began talking as fast as she could. And Laura and Bertha started giggling and shaking their heads.

At first i didn't recognize the boy who was exercising at the bar. But when he turned to face me, i was really surprised. It was Ralph Manley — the toughest linebacker on the Tidewater team. In fact, he had been one of the Tigers who tackled me at the big game.

i had heard that Ralph recently had moved to our town and would play for the Hotshots next year. i couldn't believe such a tough guy was taking ballet!

Suddenly the side door opened, and a woman entered the room like a queen. Her strides were long and graceful. Her posture was perfect. Her jet-black hair was pulled straight back into a bun. She had the lo-o-o-ongest eyelashes i had ever seen, and she wore bright red lipstick. She was gorgeous! i had no doubt that this was Madame Lezlie Camille.

"*Bon jour,* class," Madame Camille said in a deep, commanding voice that echoed throughout the room.

"*Bon jour,* Madame," the other students responded.

"Ah, I see we have a new dancer," said Madame Camille. "And what is your name?"

"My name is amy," i answered sullenly.

"Come, join us," she said, motioning to me.

Well, what else could i do? i was stuck there. So i walked across the room and stood with the others.

"Pay close attention today, class," Madame began. "Remember, it requires many years of training to become an accomplished ballet dancer."

i didn't care what the others did. The only thing i wanted to accomplish was a very fast exit from this crazy place!

"Today," Madame Camille continued, "we will be butterflies. Now, everyone up on your toes, spread your arms, and flutter around the room."

All the others started waving their arms and tippy-toeing across the floor.

"You, too, Amy!" Madame Camille commanded.

i knew i was trapped. So i raised my arms, flapped my wings like a silly bat, and started tippy-toeing around the room.

"Now that we're all relaxed, let us go to the bar and stretch our muscles," said Madame.

"All right!" i said to myself. "This is going to be easy. Coach always had us do warm-up exercises before every football practice."

i followed the others to the bar, ready to begin.

"Backs straight, tummies in, and heads held high!" ordered Madame Camille.

Holding tightly to the bar, we began to stretch our legs.

"Point your toes, Amy!" Madame Camille kept saying. "POINT YOUR TOES!"

i *did* point my toes! i pointed my toes until i thought my ankles would crack! But no matter how much i tried, i couldn't do the exercises as well as the other students.

FIRST POSITION

SECOND POSITION

13

THIRD POSITION

FOURTH POSITION

FIFTH POSITION

Then our class lined up in the center of the room.

"All dance steps in ballet are based on five foot positions," said Madame Camille. "So it is important that you learn to do these positions perfectly. Now then, everyone, stand in First Position — heels together, toes out, and legs straight."

Well, there i stood, trying to do as Madame had instructed. i must admit — First Position wasn't so hard to do. Second Position was easy too. Third and Fourth Positions were a little more difficult, but i did them fairly well.

But Fifth Position was something else! It was impossible for me to do that one correctly. When my feet were in the right places, my knees were bent. When i straightened my knees, my feet wouldn't stay where they belonged. If i got my feet and my legs lined up just right, my back swayed in and my stomach stuck out.

"Now i know how a pretzel feels!" i grumbled

"Keep trying, Amy," Madame Camille urged. "You can get it right."

By the end of class, i was exhausted. My legs were as weak as jelly. i wobbled down the stairs and out the door.

There i bumped into Robert Bunkwally, the captain of our football team. He had just come from the pet store and was carrying a goldfish in a plastic bag. When he saw me dressed in a tutu, he started to grin.

But i was not in the mood to be laughed at. i reached out, grabbed him by his collar, and snarled, "One smartaleck remark from you, Robert Bunkwally, and i'll give you a black eye and make you swallow your new pet!"

Then i turned around and hurried to the car as fast as my shaky legs would carry me.

"How do you like taking ballet?" Mom asked cheerfully.

"I'd rather eat live worms!" i replied as i plopped down in the front seat. "Madame Camille kept saying, 'Point your toes, Amy! Point your toes!' i am definitely *not* going back to ballet class next week!"

When i awakened the following morning, i yawned. Then i stretched. And then i SCREAMED! My whole body throbbed with pain! My back ached! My legs ached! My arms ached! Even my fingernails were sore.

When i finally crawled out of bed and stood up, i couldn't bend my arms or legs. So i walked stiff-legged across the room, just like Frankenstein's Monster. i decided right then and there that ballet was not for sissies. It was every bit as as tough as football.

On Monday morning my body was still sore. At school the guys on the football team were waiting for me by the front door. All of them had big grins on their faces. i knew Robert Bunkwally had told them about seeing me in my tutu.

Elizabeth Ann, of course, had spread the word throughout school that i was taking ballet lessons. And Priscilla Priss had told everyone that my "fluttering butterfly was simply dreadful!"

The next Saturday i hid under my bed. But Mom found me and dragged me to the car. i soon found myself back at the dance studio. As i limbered up at the bar that morning, Madame Camille watched every move i made.

"Point your toes, Amy!" she repeated again and again. "Straighten your legs and stretch your arms."

That woman was on my case the whole lesson!

When class ended Madame Camille said, "Amy, please stay for a minute. I want to talk to you."

Of course, Priscilla Priss and the other girls giggled with delight. They thought i was in big trouble. i overheard Priscilla say, "Amy can punt and pass a football, but she will *never* learn to point her toes correctly."

After all the students had left, Madame said, "Amy, your muscles are strong, and your coordination is excellent. But if you are going to be a dancer, you must work to stretch your muscles. And you must learn to move your arms and legs with style and grace."

"But, i don't want to be a dancer," i told her.

"Nonsense!" Madame scolded. "You have everything it takes to become a fine ballerina."

"i would rather play football," i insisted.

"And you are a very good football player," she said. "I saw you play in the big game. You were wonderful. But with some hard work, you can become a good dancer too. Someday you could be dancing a solo on center stage."

"i think my mom is waiting for me," i said, trying to change the subject.

"You think about what I've told you," Madame urged.

"i will," i replied as i hurried toward the door.

Although i tried to forget the things Madame Camille had said, i couldn't. i think it was the "solo on center stage" part that really had caught my attention.

During the next few weeks, i still groaned about having to take ballet. After all, the other students had been taking lessons for a couple of years. Even clumsy Laura could dance better than i.

"Look at what I have!" Mom said one day when i came home from school. She was holding three tickets in her hand. i was sure they were for a football game.

"Who's playing?" i asked excitedly.

"*Swan Lake*," she replied.

"Oh, no — not ballet again!" i moaned. "i don't want to see a bunch of women in bird costumes dance around on their toes!"

My parents would not listen. And since adults rule the world, i found myself sitting in the audience on the night of the ballet.

Sure enough, women dressed in bird feathers flitted back and forth across the stage. But i paid no attention to them. i thought about football instead.

Then, suddenly a guy dressed like a prince leaped onto the stage. The audience gasped, and so did i. i had never seen anyone jump so high. He looked like he was flying! Then he did it again. i was amazed!

From that point on, i got interested. i watched the whole ballet and, to my surprise, i liked it!

When i got home that night, i was all fired up and ready to go. i ran to our back yard and jumped and leaped into the air until Mom insisted i get ready for bed. For the rest of the week, i practiced three hours each day. i could hardly wait to show Madame Camille how my leaps had improved.

Saturday finally arrived. During ballet class all the others did fairly good leaps — except Laura. She couldn't run more than five steps without stumbling and sprawling flat on the floor.

At last it was my turn. i took a deep breath, ran a few steps, then leaped high into the air and soared across the room. As soon as i landed, i turned to see the others' reactions.

Everyone was astonished! Ralph raised his hands and clapped, and so did Madame. Then the others clapped too — except for Priscilla Priss. She just turned pea green with envy. i loved both the applause and seeing Priscilla's new color.

After class Ralph said to me, "Your leaps are terrific, Amy!"

"Thank you," i replied.

"I'm sorry about your arm getting broken in the big game."

"That wasn't your fault," i told him. "It took four of you guys to tackle me. But my injury did end my football-playing days."

"I know," he replied, shaking his head sadly.

"Say, Ralph, were you upset when your parents made you start taking ballet lessons?" i asked.

"No one made me take lessons," he explained. "I wanted to take them so I could learn to dance."

"Why do you want to dance?" i questioned in amazement.

"Because ballet makes me a better football player. Now I can run faster and jump higher. I used to be real clumsy."

"Like Laura?" i asked.

"Well," Ralph laughed, "no one is as clumsy as Laura."

When we arrived for class the following Saturday, Madame Camille had exciting news.

"The university is going to produce a children's ballet of *Sleeping Beauty*," she said. "Students from all the local dance studios are invited to try out. I would be so proud if even one of you got a solo part."

Everyone wanted to try out. But no one was more eager than i. i had always liked the story of *Sleeping Beauty,* and i knew the part i wanted to dance. It was my favorite part in the whole story. i was determined to do my best to get it!

For several weeks all of us worked harder in class than ever before. We practiced at home too. i did leaps across the kitchen floor and into the dining room. i used the couch as a bar when i stretched my legs. i pretended my room was a stage. As i watched myself in the mirror, i could see i was getting better and better.

Ralph's dancing really improved too; so did Elizabeth Ann's, once she stopped chattering so much. Bertha was the most graceful dancer in our group. i began to admire her. Even though she was a bit overweight, Bertha always danced beautifully.

Ralph and i began working with Laura after school. We tried to help her learn to stay on her feet and stop bumping into things. But every time we thought she had improved, she would suddenly bump into a wall or trip and fall down. Even so, she didn't give up. When Laura fell, she always got back up and tried again.

Priscilla, of course, practiced her dance steps over and over. She was never satisfied unless she did them without a flaw. When she made a mistake, she would stomp her foot and scold herself. i realized that Priscilla was under a lot of pressure. i decided it must not be easy for anyone to try to be perfect all the time.

On the morning of the try outs, Mom took me to the Performing Arts Building at the university. What a crowd! There were students from every dance studio in town.

All of us were nervous as we waited in line to be handed try-out numbers. But when i received number 13, i began to feel better.

"All right!" i said to myself. "Thirteen is my lucky football number!"

Bertha was the first one from Madame Camille's school to try out. She did a beautiful dance and ended with a graceful curtsy. i was so proud of her.

Elizabeth Ann surprised us all. She actually danced for three whole minutes without saying a single word.

When Laura stepped on stage, Ralph and i crossed our fingers. It didn't help. The first thing Laura did was trip over her own feet and plop down on her knees. The rest of her dance was a nightmare. Half way through her routine, she fell off the stage! We were afraid she had broken her neck, but she wasn't hurt.

When Laura climbed back up on the stage to finish her dance, everyone applauded her for her courage. They also laughed a bit because Laura was so funny to watch. Even the judges couldn't help but chuckle.

Ralph danced next. He was terrific! He didn't miss a step.

As for Priscilla...well...what can i say? Her dance was perfect, and she knew it. She tossed her blonde curls from side to side and smiled sweetly at the judges.

When my number was called, my heart skipped a beat. i walked to the stage and began. My routine was a difficult one with lots of leaps and fast turns. But i gave it all i had.

As i danced i kept remembering what Madame Camille had said — "Point your toes, Amy!" And i *did* point. i pointed my toes until i thought they would snap off!

When i had finished, i returned to my seat and waited. Soon all the try-outs were over. While the judges voted, i felt hot and cold, scared and excited. Sweat rolled down my forehead, and my feet were wet and slippery inside my ballet shoes.

Finally, the man who was head of the judging committee stepped on stage and announced the winners:

"The role of the prince will be danced by number 10."

Ralph rushed to the stage and claimed his part. He tried to remain cool, but i knew he was excited enough to burst.

"The good fairies will be danced by numbers 5, 7, and 9," the judge continued.

Bertha, Elizabeth Ann, and Laura ran to the stage, holding hands and giggling every step of the way.

i wasn't surprised when Laura was chosen. One of the judges had told us, "The third fairy is the clumsy one. She's always bumping into things and falling down."

i had no doubt that Laura could dance that role better than anyone else.

"Now," said the head judge, "for the role of Princess Aurora, we have chosen — dancer number 13."

"Aurora!" i exclaimed. "That's not the part i want! Who wants to be some prissy princess who sleeps through one hundred years of the ballet!"

When i glanced over at Priscilla and saw tears streaming down her face, i realized immediately who wanted to dance that role.

i rushed onto the stage and said to the judges, "i don't want to be Sleeping Beauty! i want to be the evil fairy."

The judges were so surprised, they didn't know what to do. So they huddled together and had a conference.

Finally, the head judge said, "We have decided that you, number 13, can be the evil fairy, if number 12 will agree to trade roles with you."

"Number 12!" squealed Priscilla. "That's me! Yes, I will gladly trade roles with Amy!" And she ran to the stage.

Then Priscilla did something i never thought she would do. She turned to me and, smiling through her tears, she said, "Oh, thank you, Amy. You're the best friend I ever had!"

Rehearsals for the ballet were a lot of work, but they were also great fun. By the night of the performance of *Sleeping Beauty,* all of us were well prepared to dance our parts.

As the orchestra played the overture, excitement filled the huge auditorium. At last the curtain rose, and the beautiful ballet began.

i thought the time for my solo would never arrive. But when it did, i was ready. As the music for my entrance was played, i ran onto the stage, leaped up and soared through the air. It was the longest, highest leap i had ever done. If the king and queen had not backed out of my way, i would have knocked them through the castle wall.

As soon as my feet touched the floor, i did a series of fantastic turns, spinning and whirling around and around with lightning speed. And when i waved my arms and cast my evil spell, i looked wonderfully wicked. Little kids in the audience were so frightened, they scrunched down in their chairs and shivered.

When i finished my solo, the audience went wild! People rose to their feet and shouted, "Bravo! Bravo!" They cheered and applauded so loudly, i thought the ceiling might lift off the building. i loved it! It was great to hear the sound of a cheering crowd again. i made a deep curtsy to show my appreciation.

But my biggest surprise came after the ballet had ended. When i returned to the stage and took my final bow, i could hardly believe what happened.

Robert Bunkwally stepped up and handed me a large bouquet of red roses. The flowers were beautiful. But what i liked best was the big balloon that floated on a streamer above the roses. It was shaped like a football, and written on it were the words, "FROM YOUR TEAMMATES."

"Congratulations, Amy! You've scored another touch-down!" Robert said with a big smile.

At that moment I felt like I was once again an important person. From then on, I knew I would always capitalize my "A" and my "I."

P.S. Thanks, Mom. I love you!

BOOKS FOR STUDENTS

– WINNERS OF THE NATIONAL WRITTEN

Aruna Chandrasekhar
age 9

Anika Thomas
age 13

Cara Reichel
age 15

Jonathan Kahn
age 9

Adam Moore
age 9

Leslie Ann MacKeen
age 9

Elizabeth Haidle
age 13

Amy Hagstrom
age 9

Isaac Whitlatch
age 11

Dav Pilkey
age 19

by Aruna Chandrasekhar, age 9
Houston, Texas

A touching and timely story! When the lives of many otters are threatened by a huge oil spill, a group of concerned people come to their rescue. Wonderful illustrations.
Printed Full Color
ISBN 0-933849-33-8

by Anika D. Thomas, age 13
Pittsburgh, Pennsylvania

A compelling autobiography! A young girl's heartrending account of growing up in a tough, inner-city neighborhood. The illustrations match the mood of this gripping story.
Printed Two Colors
ISBN 0-933849-34-6

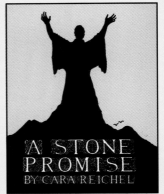

by Cara Reichel, age 15
Rome, Georgia

Elegant and eloquent! A young stonecutter vows to create a great statue for his impoverished village. But his fame almost stops him from fulfilling that promise.
Printed Two Colors
ISBN 0-933849-35-4

by Jonathan Kahn, age 9
Richmond Heights, Ohio

A fascinating nature story! Patulous, a prairie rattles searches for food, he must avoid the claws and fangs of his enemies.
Printed Full Color
ISBN 0-933849-36-2

by Adam Moore, age 9
Broken Arrow, Oklahoma

A remarkable true story! When Adam was eight years old, he fell and ran an arrow into his head. With rare insight and humor, he tells of his ordeal and his amazing recovery.
Printed Two Colors
ISBN 0-933849-24-9

by Michael Aushenker, age 19
Ithaca, New York

Chomp! Chomp! When Arthur forgets to feed his goat, the animal eats everything in sight. A very funny story — good to the last bite. The illustrations are terrific.
Printed Full Color
ISBN 0-933849-28-1

by Leslie Ann MacKeen, age 9
Winston-Salem, North Carolina

Loaded with fun and puns! When Jeremiah T. Fitz's car stops running, several animals offer suggestions for fixing it. The results are hilarious. The illustrations are charming.
Printed Full Color
ISBN 0-933849-19-2

by Elizabeth Haidle, age 13
Beaverton, Oregon

A very touching story! The gr iest Elfkin learns to cheris friendship of others after he an injured snail and befrien orphaned boy. Absolutely bea
Printed Full Color
ISBN 0-933849-20-6

by Amy Hagstrom, age 9
Portola, California

An exciting western! When a boy and an old Indian try to save a herd of wild ponies, they discover a lost canyon and see the mystical vision of the Great White Stallion.
Printed Full Color
ISBN 0-933849-15-X

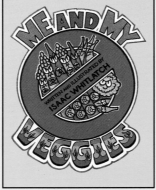

by Isaac Whitlatch, age 11
Casper, Wyoming

The true confessions of a devout vegetable hater! Isaac tells ways to avoid and dispose of the "slimy green things." His colorful illustrations provide a salad of laughter and mirth.
Printed Full Color
ISBN 0-933849-16-8

by Dav Pilkey, age 19
Cleveland, Ohio

A thought-provoking parable! Two kings halt an arms race and learn to live in peace. This outstanding book launched Dav's career. He now has seven more books published.
Printed Full Color
ISBN 0-933849-22-2

by Karen Kerber, age 12
St. Louis, Missouri

A delightfully playful book! Th is loaded with clever alliteratio gentle humor. Karen's bright ored illustrations are compos wiggly and waggly strokes of g
Printed Full Color
ISBN 0-933849-29-X

To obtain Contest Rules, send a self-addressed, business-size envelope, stamped with .58 postage,

yna Miller, age 19
anesville, Ohio

funniest Halloween ever! When
mer the Rabbit takes all the
s, his friends get even. Their
ious scheme includes a haunted
se and mounds of chocolate.
d Full Color
0-933849-37-0

by Lauren Peters, age 7
Kansas City, Missouri

The Christmas that almost wasn't!
When Santa Claus takes a vacation,
Mrs. Claus and the elves go on strike.
Toys aren't made. Cookies aren't
baked. Super illustrations.
Printed Full Color
ISBN 0-933849-25-7

by Michael Cain, age 11
Annapolis, Maryland

A glorious tale of adventure!To
become a knight, a young man must
face a beast in the forest, a spell-
binding witch, and a giant bird that
guards a magic oval crystal.
Printed Full Color
ISBN 0-933849-26-5

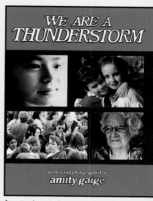

by Amity Gaige, age 16
Reading, Pennsylvania

A lyrical blend of poetry and pho-
tographs! Amity's sensitive poems
offer thought-provoking ideas and
amusing insights. This lovely book
is one to be savored and enjoyed.
Printed Full Color
ISBN 0-933849-27-3

eidi Salter, age 19
rkeley, California

ky and wonderful! To save her
imagination, a young girl must
ront the Great Grey Grimly
elf. The narrative is filled with
nse. Vibrant illustrations.
d Full Color
0-933849-21-4

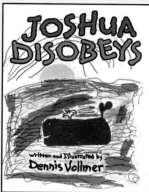

by Dennis Vollmer, age 6
Grove, Oklahoma

A baby whale's curiosity gets him
into a lot of trouble. GUINNESS
BOOK OF RECORDS lists Dennis as
the youngest author/illustrator of a
published book.
Printed Full Color
ISBN 0-933849-12-5

by Lisa Gross, age 12
Santa Fe, New Mexico

A touching story of self-esteem! A
puppy is laughed at because of his
unusual appearance. His search for
acceptance is told with sensitivity
and humor. Wonderful illustrations.
Printed Full Color
ISBN 0-933849-13-3

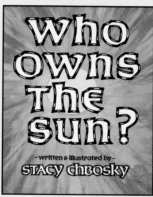

by Stacy Chbosky, age 14
Pittsburgh, Pennsylvania

A powerful plea for freedom! This
emotion-packed story of a young
slave touches an essential part of
the human spirit. Made into a film
by Disney Educational Productions.
Printed Full Color
ISBN 0-933849-14-1

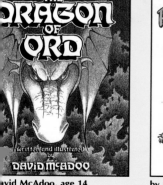

vid McAdoo, age 14
ringfield, Missouri

citing intergalactic adventure!
e distant future, a courageous
r defends a kingdom from a
n from outer space. Astound-
epia illustrations.
d Duotone
0-933849-23-0

by Bonnie-Alise Leggat, age 8
Culpeper, Virginia

Amy J. Kendrick wants to play football, but her mother wants her to
become a ballerina. Their clash of
wills creates hilarious situations.
Clever, delightful illustrations!
Printed Full Color
ISBN 0-933849-39-7

by Lisa Kirsten Butenhoff, age 13
Woodbury, Minnesota

The people of a Russian village face
the winter without warm clothes or
enough food. Then their lives are
improved by a young girl's gifts. A
tender story with lovely illustrations.
Printed Full Color
ISBN 0-933849-40-0

by Jennifer Brady, age 17
Columbia, Missouri

When poachers capture a pride of
lions, a native boy tries to free
the animals. A skillfully told story.
Glowing illustrations illuminate this
African adventure.
Printed Full Color
ISBN 0-933849-41-9

NTEST FOR STUDENTS, Landmark Editions, Inc., P.O. Box 4469, Kansas City, MO 64127.

Jayna Miller
age 19

Lauren Peters
age 7

Michael Cain
age 11

Heidi Salter
age 19

Amity Gaige
age 16

Dennis Vollmer
age 6

Lisa Gross
age 12

Stacy Chbosky
age 14

Karen Kerber
age 12

David McAdoo
age 14

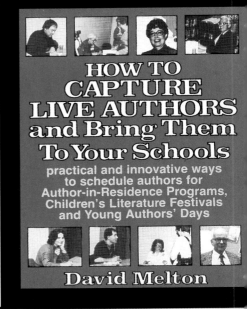